W9-BSR-318

Look! Look! Look! at Sculpture

Written and illustrated by **Nancy Elizabeth Wallace**
with **Linda K. Friedlaender**

Marshall Cavendish Children

One afternoon, three tiny mice came out of their tiny mouse house. They climbed up onto the long table Mrs. Bigley used for her desk. Alexander and Kat spied a card.

Alexander read:

Celebrate sculpture at the museum!

Four Rectangles with Four Oblique Circles, 1966
Barbara Hepworth, sculptor
Material: slate

CALDER   HESSE   OLDENBURG   MOORE   NOGUCHI
SAINT-GAUDENS   NEVELSON

CALDER   MICHELANGELO   LIPCHITZ   RODIN   SAINT-GAUDENS   BRANCUSI

"Let's go!" said Kat.

William III, ca. 1700 or ca. 1750

So off they went.

The Museum Shop

Celebrate Sculpture!

ART MUSEUM

When the mice got to the museum, they hid behind a broom and bucket until the building closed for the night. Then they tiptoed into the gallery.

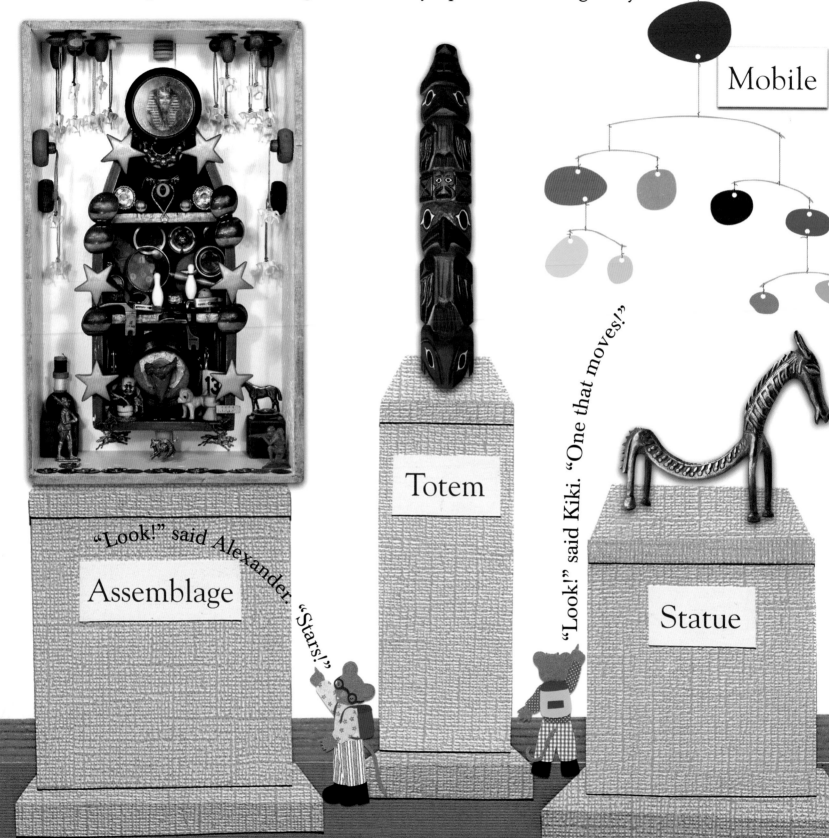

Mobile

Totem

Statue

Assemblage

"Look!" said Alexander. "Stars!"

"Look!" said Kiki. "One that moves!"

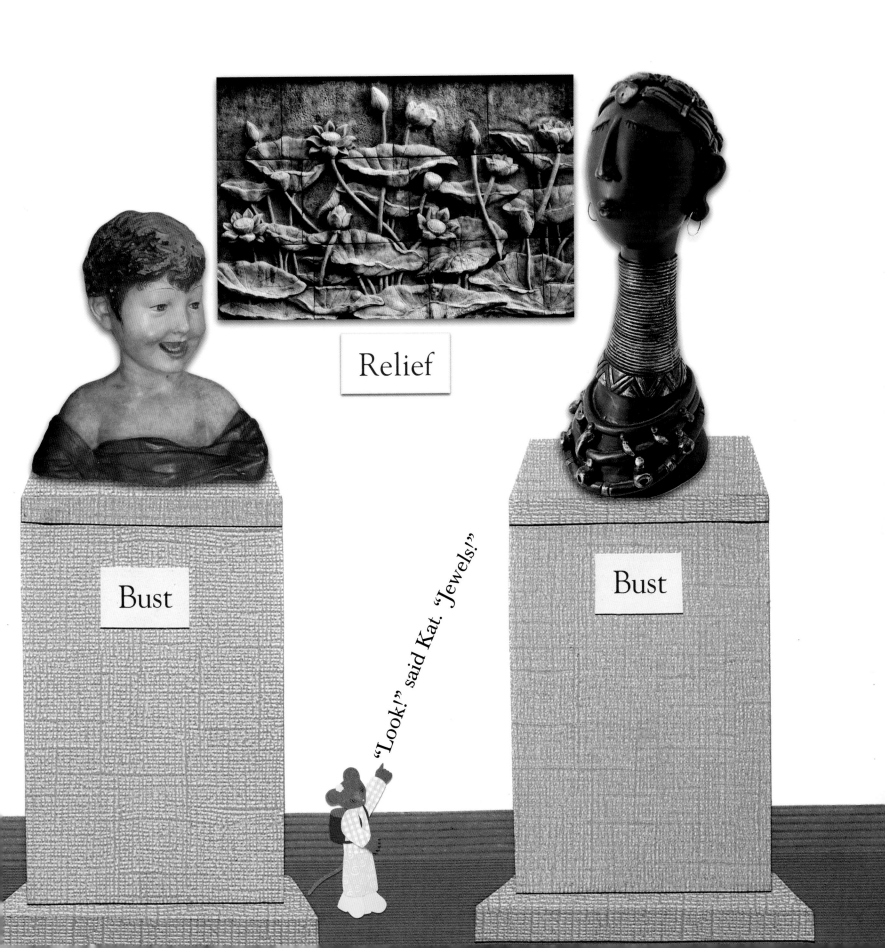

Bust

Relief

Bust

"Look!" said Kat. "Jewels!"

"There it is!" they whispered. "The sculpture from the invitation."

They scooched up the pedestal.

"Two shapes are short and two are tall," said Kat.

"It's bigger than we are!" said Kiki.

"It's made of slate. It must be very heavy," said Alexander.

"And I see spaces between the shapes!" said Alexander.

Kat said, "I see spaces *in* the shapes!"

Kiki said, "I see four smooth, shiny, crescent-moon shapes! Let's . . .

. . . **LOOK** some more."

They clasped their hands behind their backs and
did a museum walk around the sculpture.

They looked at the sides.

They looked at the back.

They looked at the front.

"It feels like a forest," said Kat.

"I think it's a family," said Kiki.

"The holes are like portholes on a boat," said Alexander.
"Let's . . .

. . . sketch!"

They took pencils and pads out of their packs.

They started drawing.

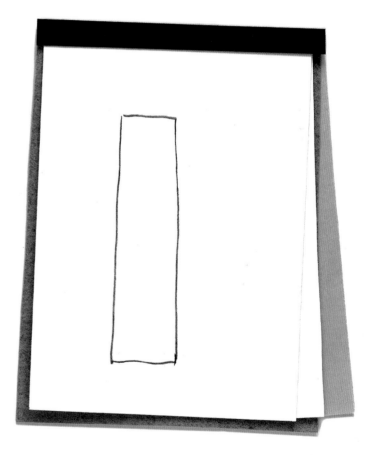

"Let's add to our sketches!" said Kiki.

She drew more lines and added shading.

Alexander and Kat did too.

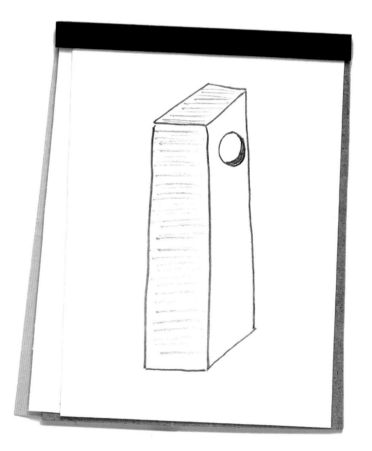

"Now our sketches don't look flat," said Kat.

"The sketches look 3-D!" they squeaked.

"Just like the sculpture is," said Alexander.

"3-D!" Kat said again. "What if . . .

. . . we each make a clay sculpture!"

They reached into their packs and pulled out clay.

"One standing alone," said Kat.

"Look!" said Alexander. "Mine with yours. They're saying hello!"

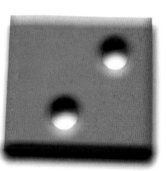

"Now it's a group sculpture! And mine looks good enough to eat!" said Kiki.

"I'll make one more," said Kiki.
"And then we'll have four."

"What if . . ." said Alexander.

"... we add to the fourth one."

Alexander worked on the front.
"Look! Squiggles!"

Kiki worked on the back.
"Look! Bumps!"

Kat worked on the sides. "Look! X marks!"

"Texture!" they shouted.

They looked at what they had created.
Then Kat said, "Let's take turns . . .

. . . arranging them."

"Ta-da," said Kat.

"When I put them this way," said Kiki,
"the yellow one looks lonely."

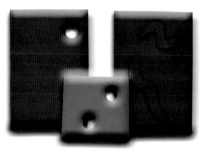

"Look at them this way," said Alexander.

"Whooaaa!" said Kat.

"This way feels like music," said Alexander.

de

deee"

"dum

dum

"Now they look like they are dancing!" said Kiki.

"What if . . ." said Alexander . . .

"... we make shapes that look like the holes!"

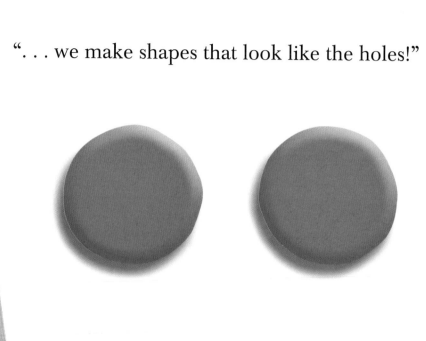

"Let's cut one in half," said Kat.

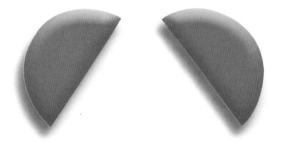

"Let's roll out the other," said Kiki, "and put some shapes together."

"**LOOK!**" they squealed.

Suddenly, they heard footsteps. They had just
enough time to pack up, climb down, and scamper out
the entrance door before it was the people's turn to
LOOK! LOOK! LOOK! at sculpture!

The Bigleys
123 Green Crescent Place
Orange, OR 97808

Italia

Postage

Recycled Paper

Look! Look! Look! Some More!

Sculpture is three-dimensional, 3-D.
Sculpture can be made of
   different materials,
be different colors,
be small or BIG or in between,
be heavy or light
   or else *look* heavy or light,
   even if it isn't.

Fish: carved wood, Africa

Origami Figure: paper, Canada

Mobile: metal, USA

Totem: carved wood and paint, Alaska

Leapfrog: carved wood and paint, USA

Antique Bust of a Boy: painted clay, Italy

Two Figurines: stone, ancient

Water Lilies Relief: carved stone, India

Rhino Head: copper, Congo

William III: lead, England

Sculpture can have a surface that is textured or smooth, shiny or dull.
Sculpture can move, stand alone, or be in a group; be outside or inside.

Assemblage: found objects and wooden box, USA

Cycladic Figure: stone, Greece

Cat: basalt/labradorite, Egypt

Scissors: glass, USA

Bust of a Woman: carved wood and paint, Africa

Horse: bronze, ancient

Four Rectangles with Four Oblique Circles: slate, England

The Commuter: carved tree root and paint, USA

Two Eskimos: soapstone, Eskimo

Coatimundi: carved wood and paint, Mexico

Woman Figurine: metal, USA

Find sculpture to **LOOK** at
— in a house, at a museum, in a park, at school, on the street in a city or town, in front of a building, in a garden . . . everywhere!

Create Paper SHAPE Sculptures!

A sculpture is three-dimensional, 3-D. You can walk all the way around it. Some sculptures make you think about the spaces in the sculpture and the space around it.

You will need:

Sturdy colored, white, or black paper or card stock
    (recycled paper or light cardboard works well, too)
scissors
pencil and ruler
shoe box or other box with a lid
paper punch (optional)
round jar lids (optional)

Step 1

Use the pencil and ruler to draw or trace squares on the card stock.

Cut them out.

small   *medium*   *large*   *larger*

Step 2

Fold the squares, corner **a** to corner **c**, to make triangles that will stand up.

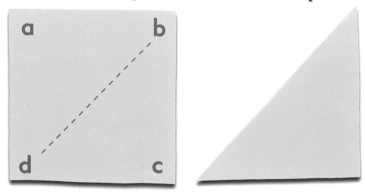

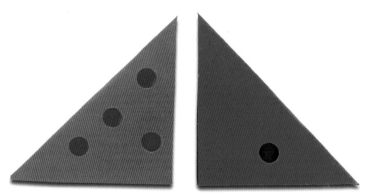

(Optional: Punch a hole(s) in one or more of the triangle sides with a paper punch.)

Step 3

CREATE! Have FUN!

Arrange the triangles in lots of different ways to create paper sculptures.

Take museum walks around your sculptures.

Look at . . . . the front . . . the sides . . . the back.

(Optional: Trace around different sizes of jar lids. Cut out the circles and fold them. Use the half-circles alone or with the triangles to create more paper sculptures.)

Choose one sculpture that you especially like. What does it make you think about? Feel? What title would you give your sculpture? Write a story or poem about your sculpture.

You can use the box for a pedestal and then add to and store your paper shapes inside. That way, you can create paper sculptures again and again!

The Sculptures

Jacket and Throughout

"Four Rectangles with Four Oblique Circles," 1966, slate, Barbara Hepworth, 1903–1975; overall: 14 x 25 ⅞ x 7 ¼ inches (35.6 x 65.7 x 18.4 cm), Yale Center for British Art, gift of Susan Morse Hilles; courtesy of Sophie Bowness and the Barbara Hepworth Estate, © Bowness, Hepworth Estate. Photo: Richard Caspole, Yale Center for British Art.

Sculpture Book

"Leapfrog," carved wood and paint, William Kirkpatrick, USA; courtesy of Jerry Theise.

"Fish," carved wood, artist unknown, Africa; Shutterstock.

Desk

"Woman Figurine," metal, artist unknown, USA; Shutterstock.

Outside

"William III," ca. 1700 or ca. 1750, lead, John Nost the Elder, before 1660–1711/1712 or John Cheere, 1709–1787; overall: 70 x 33 x 29 inches (177.8 x 83.8 x 73.7 cm), Yale Center for British Art, Paul Mellon Collection. Photo: Richard Caspole, Yale Center for British Art.

Museum Shop Window

"Scissors," glass, Henry Kudlinski, USA; courtesy of Nancy E. Wallace.

"Two Figurines," stone, ancient, artist unknown; Shutterstock.

"Rhino Head," copper, artist unknown, Congo; courtesy of Linda K. Friedlaender.

"Cat," basalt/labradorite, ancient, Egypt; Shutterstock.

"Origami Figure," paper, J. Wu, Canada; courtesy of Linda K. Friedlaender.

"Cycladic Figure," stone, ancient, Greece; courtesy of Linda K. Friedlaendar.

"Two Eskimos," soapstone, Annie Niviazie, Canadian Eskimo; courtesy of Sally Cole-Whiffen.

"Coatimundi," carved wood and paint, artist unknown, Mexico; Shutterstock.

Inside the Museum

"Assemblage, Memory Box # 3 for Lisa Mendel," found objects and wooden box, Harvee Riggs, USA; courtesy of Diane Chodkowski.

"Totem," carved wood and paint, H. Rudick, Alaska; courtesy of Sally Cole-Wiffen.

"Mobile," metal, artist unknown, USA; Shutterstock.

"Horse," bronze, ancient, artist unknown; Shutterstock.

"Antique Bust of a Boy," painted clay, artist unknown, Italy; courtesy of Alexine Wallace.

"Water Lilies Relief," carved stone, artist unknown, India; Shutterstock.

"Bust of a Woman," carved wood and paint, artist unknown, Africa; Shutterstock.

Back of Jacket

"The Commuter," carved tree root and paint, Carlyle Alexander, USA; courtesy of Alexine Wallace.

Paintings on the Museum Wall

"Seascape," by Nancy Elizabeth Wallace, courtesy of the artist.

"Aloft," by Claudia Oppenheim Cameron, courtesy of the artist.

"The Cottage," by Carrie Banks, courtesy of the Banks family.

"Windmill Palms," by Alise Nielson, courtesy of Nancy E. Wallace.

Barbara Hepworth

(1903–1975) was an important and innovative sculptor of the twentieth century. She was born in Wakefield, England, studied art and sculpture in London, and lived most of her adult life in Cornwall, on the west coast of England. She liked exploring the shoreline, cliffs, caves, rock formations, boulders, and hilltops of the rugged British landscape, and she had a large collection of driftwood. All these natural shapes influenced the look of her sculptures. She was one of the earliest sculptors to pierce, or make holes, in her solid forms in order to study spaces within shapes. She worked mostly in slate, wood, bronze, and marble.

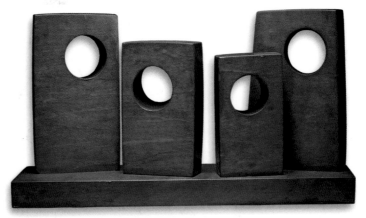

We are deeply grateful to Dr. Sophie Bowness, Sir Alan Bowness, and the Hepworth Estate for their kind permission to use "Four Rectangles with Four Oblique Circles," 1966, in *Look! Look! Look! at Sculpture.*

                    –N.E.W. and L.K.F

For Margery, Anahid, and Virginia,
my ARTFUL friends, with love
–*N.E.W.*

For Eron, Alexander, Emma, Olivia, and Ari, with love
–*L.K.F.*

Special thanks to Melissa Fournier, Maria Singer, Lyn Rose, Ilana Harris-Babou, and Michelle Andreani

Jacket sculpture: "Four Rectangles with Four Oblique Circles," Barbara Hepworth, 1966
Text and illustrations copyright © 2012 by Nancy Elizabeth Wallace

Marshall Cavendish Corporation, 99 White Plains Road, Tarrytown, NY 10591
www.marshallcavendish.us/kids

Library of Congress Cataloging-in-Publication Data

Wallace, Nancy Elizabeth.
Look! look! look! at sculpture / written and illustrated by Nancy Elizabeth Wallace with Linda K. Friedlaender. – 1st ed.
p. cm.
Summary: Three mice "borrow" a postcard which is a reproduction of a sculpture,
and from it they learn about color, pattern, line, and shape.
Includes instructions for making paper sculptures.
ISBN 978-0-7614-6132-6 (hardcover) – ISBN 978-0-7614-6133-3 (ebook)
[1. Postcards–Fiction. 2. Sculpture–Fiction. 3. Art–Fiction. 4. Mice–Fiction.] I. Friedlaender, Linda, ill. II. Title.
PZ7.W15875Loo 2012
[E]–dc23
2011029156

The illustrations are rendered in paper, photographs, and colored pencils.

Book design by Virginia Pope
Editor: Margery Cuyler

Printed in China (E)
First edition
1 3 5 6 4 2